S0-AXC-659

50d

SIMPKIN

Quentin Blake

VIKING

for ecc

VIKING
Published by the Penguin Group
Penguin Books USA Inc., 375 Hudson Street, New York, New York 10014, U.S.A
Penguin Books Ltd, 27 Wrights Lane, London W8 5TZ, England
Penguin Books Australia Ltd, Ringwood, Victoria, Australia
Penguin Books Canada Ltd, 10 Alcorn Avenue, Toronto, Ontario, Canada M4V 3B2
Penguin Books (N.Z.) Ltd, 182-190 Wairau Road, Auckland 10, New Zealand

Penguin Books Ltd, Registered Offices: Harmondsworth, Middlesex, England

First published in the United Kingdom by Jonathan Cape Ltd.,
a division of Random House UK Ltd., 1993
First published in the United States of America by Viking,
a division of Penguin Books USA Inc., 1994

1 3 5 7 9 10 8 6 4 2

Copyright © Quentin Blake, 1993
All rights reserved

Library of Congress Catalog Card Number: 93-60582
ISBN 0-670-85371-2
Printed in Hong Kong
Set in Horley Old Style

Without limiting the rights under copyright reserved above, no part of this
publication may be reproduced, stored in or introduced into a retrieval system,
or transmitted, in any form or by any means (electronic, mechanical,
photocopying, recording or otherwise), without the prior written permission
of both the copyright owner and the above publisher of this book.

Here is
SIMPKIN

Simpkin
ONCE

and Simpkin
TWICE

Simpkin NASTY

Simpkin NICE

Simpkin FAST

and Simpkin SLOW

Simpkin HIGH

and Simpkin
LOW

Simpkin
ROUND and ROUND
the chairs

Simpkin UP

and DOWN the stairs

Simpkin THIN

and Simpkin FAT

Simpkin THIS

and Simpkin THAT

Simpkin WEAK

and Simpkin STRONG

Simpkin SHORT

and Simpkin LONG

Simpkin SMOOTH

and Simpkin ROUGH

and Simpkin
THAT IS QUITE ENOUGH

Simpkin WARM

and Simpkin CHILLY

Simpkin SENSIBLE

and
SILLY

And

sometimes

when

we

stand

and

call

Simpkin

JUST

NOT

THERE

AT

ALL

8600 - 1